ABOUT THE AUTHOR

Christopher Pike was born in New York, but grew up in Los Angeles, where he still lives. Prior to becoming a writer he worked in a factory, painted houses and programmed computers. His hobbies include astronomy, meditating, running and making sure his books are prominently displayed in his local bookshop. As well as being a best-selling children's writer, he is also the author of three novels for adults.

Spooksville

Spooksville

THE THING
IN THE CLOSET

Christopher Pike

Hodder
Children's
Books

a division of Hodder Headline plc

First published in Great Britain in 1997
by Hodder Children's Books
a division of Hodder Headline plc
338 Euston Road
London NW1 3BH

10 9 8 7 6 5 4 3 2 1

A Catalogue record for this book is available from the British Library

ISBN 0 340 68624 3

Typeset by Avon Dataset Ltd, Bidford-on-Avon, Warks

Printed and bound in Great Britain by
Cox & Wyman Ltd, Reading, Berks

One

Cindy Makey awoke with a start. But she hadn't heard a noise. Apart from the soft pounding of her heart, her bedroom was completely quiet. Turning her head, she glanced at her clock. It was three in the morning, and outside it was dark. Briefly, she wondered why she had woken up at all. She was pretty sure she had been sleeping deeply. She was just about to roll over and go back to sleep when she noticed the faint green glow coming from her closet door.

Cindy sat up and stared at it.

Like most people, Cindy had always been a little afraid of a dark closet. Especially now, in the middle of the night, when the closet door was slightly ajar. There was just something about the darkness inside the closet – it was as if it were a portal into horrors unimagined. At the same time, she didn't much like getting into bed in the dark. She was always worried a hand would reach out and grab her ankle and drag her under the bed. What would happen next would be just too awful to contemplate.

Of course Cindy was twelve years old, a big girl, and she knew these fears were ridiculous. There was nothing either in her closet or under her bed that could hurt her. Really, she should have outgrown these fears long ago.

Then again, this was Spooksville.

Where kids disappeared without warning all the time.

And there was something strange glowing in her closet.

That was a fact. Not imagination.

Cindy rubbed her eyes and leaned forward on her bed and studied the light further. It was the weirdest green colour. Not like grass or trees, more like something sickly – the green-tinted skin of a dying patient. For a moment Cindy almost believed there was an odour of decay in the room, but then she realised that was her imagination.

'But what could it be?' she whispered aloud.

There was really nothing she could do but examine it closer.

Get out of bed and walk over to the closet.

But she didn't want to do that.

Not this second at least.

Cindy hoped it was her flashlight. That somehow it had slipped off the shelf in the closet and turned itself on. Of course the flashlight did not give off a green beam, but she wondered if the light could be shining through a green sweater or something. The only trouble was, she didn't own a green sweater. And her one and only green shirt was in her chest of drawers, not in the closet. For that matter, she didn't even think her flashlight was still in the closet. She had used it a couple of days ago in the garage, looking for loose change, and she thought she had left it there. No, this weird glow had to be something else.

'Like what?' she muttered.

Cindy reached over and tried to turn on the lamp beside her bed. For some reason it wouldn't come on. She fiddled with the switch for a few moments before giving up. Was it possible, she asked herself, that the green glow was somehow affecting her lamp? It seemed unlikely, and yet her lamp had been working a few hours ago when she had gone to bed. She wondered if the green glow liked the dark. If it *needed* the dark.

She wondered what it wanted with her.

'This is stupid,' she chided herself aloud. 'It is just a light. It is not alive. It can't hurt me.'

She hoped it couldn't, boy did she. Now that she had mentally exhausted everything that it could be, she knew she finally had to have a closer look at it. How could she go back to sleep without checking it out? For all she knew the green glow would transform itself into a green hungry monster while she was asleep and then eat her alive. Things like that happened in Spooksville, at least according to her friend, Sally Wilcox. Ordinarily Cindy didn't believe most of what Sally said but at the moment even Sally's darkest and most disturbing ravings seemed possible.

For a second Cindy considered calling Sally.

Or Adam Freeman, another best friend.

But she was afraid they might think she was a chicken.

'I am a chicken,' Cindy said to herself. 'Adam would have jumped out of bed the moment he saw the glow. He's not afraid of anything.'

Cindy sort of liked Adam.

Quite a bit, really, even though he didn't know it.

Cindy slowly climbed out of her bed. The floor was cold. She trembled as she walked towards the closet. The green glow seemed to brighten slightly at her approach.

'Please don't hurt me,' Cindy whispered as she drew close to the closet. The door was only slightly ajar. She could just see inside the closet. The green glow had turned her clothes all green, as well as her shoes and hats. Cindy was a big hat lover. Usually, she couldn't wait till the weather turned cold so that she could wear one. But seeing how sickly green they were right now, through the crack in the door, she wondered if she would ever wear them again. It seemed as if this glow was actually sinking into the material. Into her skin, even, as she stood outside the closet. The light itself felt cold, as if it were being generated by a huge block of alien ice.

Yet Cindy could see no source of the light.

It just seemed to come from the back of the closet.

To get a better look she needed to open the door all the way. And she didn't want to do that. She didn't want to let whatever was inside out into her bedroom.

'But it's not alive,' she told herself again. 'It can't hurt me.'

Cindy took hold of the door knob.

With trembling fingers, she pulled the door open a little bit further.

The green glow went out.

Cindy yanked the door all the way open.

The closet was completely dark. The way it was supposed to be.

'Hello?' Cindy called, feeling stupid.

No one called back.

Behind her, beside the bed, her lamp popped on. The light made her jump. Thank goodness it wasn't green. Cindy used the light from the lamp to explore the closet further. Her clothes, her shoes, her hats – nothing seemed out of place. Yet there must have been something that gave off the light, she thought. She just couldn't figure out what it was.

Cindy left her bedroom and peeked in on her sleeping brother and mother. There didn't seem to be any green glow in their closets. Returning to her bedroom, she checked her closet one more time. Still nothing, and she was glad there wasn't. Yet the mystery remained and that disturbed her even more.

Eventually Cindy returned to bed and turned off the light.

It was not long before she was asleep.

Too fast asleep to notice that the closet door she had so carefully closed had popped open. Too fast asleep to see the green glow return.

Too fast asleep to see the faint face form in the middle of the glow.

A face that was definitely not human.

Two

The next morning, Saturday, Cindy sat with her friends in their favourite doughnut shop. It was their custom, now that term had started again, to eat breakfast together each Saturday and Sunday morning. Adam and Sally were there, and so were Watch and Bryce Pool. Adam was the shortest one in the group, as well as their leader. He was very smart and full of good ideas. Sally was practically as tall as the other guys, and was always talking. Her wit was biting. Watch was perhaps the quietest. He was called Watch because he always wore four watches at the same time. No one knew his real name. Bryce was the most dynamic one in the group, or maybe just the most arrogant. Cindy loved them all very much.

Plus they had a newcomer at breakfast, Tira Jones. They had only met her when the No Ones had tried to invade Spooksville. The No Ones had actually been ancient souls from a distant planet who had got trapped on earth. They had floated around like huge balls of light. They had been wiped out in an electric storm the gang had helped create with a magic potion from the town witch.

One of these No Ones had possessed Tira's body two hundred years ago. As a result, she had not aged in all that time. Together they had managed to drive the invading soul from her body, but to this day Tira had no memory of every being fused with the No Ones. For her, it seemed as if two hundred years had passed in a moment. She was still adjusting to life in modern-day Spooksville. She lived with a foster family that Watch had found for her. Because this couple didn't have children, they had been overjoyed to meet Tira. She seemed to like them as well. Besides being incredibly beautiful, with long dark hair and deep blue eyes, Tira was very sweet. She was so kind that even Sally had to like her, and Sally did not readily warm to pretty girls.

Cindy was trying to explain to all of them the green glow.

'It seemed to come from the back of the closet,' she said. 'It was unlike any light I have seen before. The green was like something an alien ship might give off. It wasn't even that bright, but it seemed to sink into all my clothes.'

'What do you mean sink into them?' Adam asked, chewing on a doughnut.

'The light seemed to stain the clothes is what I mean,' Cindy said.

'But were they stained?' Watch asked, sipping a carton of milk.

'No,' Cindy said. 'When I stepped to the closet door and opened it all the way, the light went off. Then everything was as it had always been. But I couldn't find a source for the light.'

'You might have just been dreaming,' Sally said.

'I know the difference between a dream and reality,' Cindy said.

'In this town there often isn't much difference,' Sally said.

Cindy shook her head. 'This was real. I saw it with my own eyes. What do you guys think it could have been?'

'I have never heard of anything like this before,' Watch said.

'Perhaps there is an interdimensional portal in your bedroom closet,' Bryce suggested. 'There's one in the cemetery.'

'And Cindy's bedroom is like a morgue,' Sally added.

'This was not like the Secret Path,' Cindy said, referring to the magical portal that they had used before to travel in time and other dimensions.

'How can you be sure?' Bruce asked. 'You say the light had no obvious source. Maybe its source was another dimension, that for some reason closed when you opened the door.'

Cindy was thoughtful. 'I suppose that is possible.'

'How did this green light feel?' Tira asked. Because she was still getting used to the modern world, she spent more time watching and listening

12

than giving suggestions. But they had all learned from experience that Tira was intuitive. She often knew things she had no way of knowing. The others suspected this ability was a lingering effect of her having been with a No One for two hundred years. They didn't say that to her, however, since she seemed reluctant to talk about the No Ones at all.

'What do you mean?' Cindy asked.

'Did the light feel good?' Tira asked.

Cindy hesitated. 'No. It felt cold. It felt . . . evil.'

Tira nodded. 'I thought so.'

'Wait a second,' Sally said. 'How can a light feel evil?'

Cindy shrugged. 'Maybe evil is too strong a word. But it definitely didn't feel like a good thing. I was glad when it vanished.' She paused and glanced at Tira. 'Why did you think it was evil?'

Tira's eyes were far away, as they often were.

'I just felt it was not good,' she said quietly.

Cindy smiled nervously. 'Now you're scaring me.'

'Maybe a little fear is good,' Adam said. 'Maybe

Tira or Sally should sleep over with you tonight.'

'I don't want to sleep over at her house,' Sally said. 'Not if she has green goo dripping out of her closet.'

'I told you, it was green light,' Cindy said. 'Anyway, I don't want you to sleep over.' She paused, and added, 'I'll be all right.'

'Are you sure?' Tira asked. 'I don't mind staying with you.'

Cindy forced a smile. 'I'm not afraid of a little green glow.'

'But it is possible this glow is the tip of the iceberg,' Watch said. 'A radioactive nuclear bomb can give off a faint green glow. It can also wipe out an entire city. I would like to examine your closet, Cindy, right now.'

Cindy stood up. 'That's fine. I think my mother and brother are out shopping. Now is a good time.'

The gang gathered around the closet, as if peering into a strange realm, and yet they saw nothing unusual. The rear of the closet seemed as sub-stantial as ever and none of the clothes showed any

14

lingering effect of the glow. Sally picked up one of Cindy's woollen hats and tried it on.

'How do I look?' she asked, posing for the others.

'Go for the whole effect and pull it down over your face,' Bryce suggested.

Sally made a face. 'Very funny. Cindy, I didn't know you had so many hats.'

'It is a hobby of mine to collect them,' Cindy admitted.

'I like to collect watches,' Watch said.

'Who would have guessed?' Sally said.

Adam stepped into the closet and felt along the walls.

'There don't seem to be any hidden trap doors,' he said, running his fingers along the wood. 'At least none that I can feel.'

Watch nodded. 'But that is not necessarily good news. It might mean the light has a supernatural origin.'

Cindy cringed. 'Are you saying my closet is haunted?'

'Not necessarily,' Watch replied, turning to Tira. 'Do you feel anything strange here?'

15

Tira stood still for a moment.

'No,' she said finally. 'But it is not dark. That might make a difference.'

'Why do you say that?' Cindy asked.

'You mentioned on the way over here that your lamp went out while the green light was there,' said Adam. 'It only came on when the glow left. There might be a connection.'

'Maybe you just need a nightlight,' Sally said to Cindy. 'Sissy.'

'A battery-powered nightlight might not be a bad idea,' Watch said.

'Why battery-powered?' Cindy asked.

Watch shrugged. 'The glow appeared to short the wall socket the last time.'

'Personally I think we are making a big fuss about nothing more than a bad dream,' said Sally, trying on another one of Cindy's hats. This one was like a Girl Scout's cap, only the emblem was missing.

'But you're the one who is always warning us about every little omen,' Cindy said.

'Maybe I am getting more sensible in my old age,' Sally said.

'I don't know,' Adam said. 'I don't like leaving you alone tonight, Cindy.'

Cindy put on a brave front. 'That's not necessary. If the green glow returns, I'll call you immediately, Adam.'

He nodded reluctantly. 'I'll be over straight away.'

'Sounds like true love to me,' Sally said, with a smirk on her face.

Three

That night, unsurprisingly Cindy had trouble falling asleep. She had not told her mother or little brother about the light. When it came to fighting ugly aliens and other evil forces of darkness, the gang usually kept to themselves. Cindy could hear her mother and brother sleeping peacefully in their adjoining bedrooms. She only wished she could do likewise. But she could not keep her eyes off the closet, even though she had closed the door firmly. She had even propped her desk chair against the door knob, to prevent anything from trying to break into her room. She was just being foolish, she knew, but she wanted to be safe.

But safe from what?

She wished she had bought a nightlight.

Cindy hadn't even lain down yet, at least not for any length of time. Each time she relaxed she thought she heard a faint sound from the direction of the closet and it would make her sit up with a start. Of course each time there would be nothing there. Yet it did not stop her from jumping up the next time as well.

'This is stupid,' she said aloud. 'I'll be exhausted in the morning. And I have to study all day tomorrow.'

She glanced at the clock.

It was already one in the morning.

Outside the window it was very dark. Something scratched at the glass but it was only the branch of a tree, moved by the wind. Gathering her blanket close to her chin, she tried lying down again.

It was then she noticed the green glow.

Coming from beneath her closet door.

Cindy practically flew out of her bed, she sat up so quickly.

She reached for the lamp switch. But the lamp

would not go on. She grabbed the phone beside her bed, and was grateful to hear the dialling tone. But she had trouble dialling Adam's number in the dark, in her terror. It was true, the green glow seemed much more horrible tonight. Finally, though, his phone began to ring. It took Adam three long rings before he answered. He sounded sleepy.

'Hello?' he said.

'Adam!' she hissed. 'It's back!'

He took a moment. 'The green glow?'

'Yeah! It's on right now in my closet.'

'Wow.'

'What should I do? Can you really come over?'

'Yeah, I can come. I can be there in ten minutes. But don't do anything until I get there. Stay away from the closet.'

'Should I call the others?'

Adam considered. 'Not yet. Let me look at it.'

'All right.'

'Stay cool, Cindy. It's only a light. It can't hurt you.'

'Then why do you want me to stay away from it?'

21

He hesitated. 'You can never be too careful in this town. I'm on my way.'

They exchanged goodbyes and then Cindy was alone again, with the green glow. Even though the closet door was closed, it definitely seemed brighter than the previous night. That just scared her all the more. Yet she was hesitant to leave the room, to just leave the glow to its own devices. Even though she got out of bed, she found herself pacing almost helplessly in front of the closet. It was if the green glow had some kind of sick hold over her. She was afraid to be near it and afraid to let it out of her sight.

Then she heard a faint sound.

A faint rustling. Inside the closet.

'Oh no,' she gasped.

It was alive. Maybe that meant it was hungry.

Summoning her courage, Cindy stepped to the closet door and checked to make sure the top of her chair was wedged tightly against the door knob. Every muscle in her body quivered. There was definitely something moving inside the closet. Although it was not making much noise, it sounded big. It even sounded as if it was rubbing up against the door.

Trying to get out. Trying to get to her.

Cindy let go of the chair and took a step back.

'Please hurry, Adam,' she whispered.

Then there was a sharp bang inside the closet.

A bang against the door. The chair rattled.

Every nerve in her body rattled.

'Oh,' Cindy moaned.

Another hard bang. The chair fell to the side.

Cindy stood frozen in terror.

The green glow blazed from under the door.

Tears rolled down Cindy's face.

'Somebody help me,' she cried softly.

But no one heard her. No one helped her.

The closet door slowly opened.

The thing came out of the closet. The horrible thing.

And it grabbed Cindy. Grabbed her as she went to scream.

Then it took her away. Back into the closet.

Down into a dark place where no one could hear her scream.

Four

When Adam reached Cindy's house, he did not knock on the front door. He was afraid of disturbing her mother or little brother. It was an unspoken code among them that they did not bring family into their private business, which largely consisted of staying alive in Spooksville. Instead, Adam slipped down the side of the house and knocked lightly on Cindy's bedroom window. The night was cool and she had her window shut tight. Still, he was surprised when, after a minute, she did not answer. He knocked again and waited. Finally, getting worried, he forced the window open from the outside.

A glance inside showed no Cindy.

Quickly he jumped up and climbed inside.

The first thing he noticed about her bedroom was that her closet door was lying all the way open and that her desk chair lay on its side beside the closet. Almost as if the chair had been pushed over. There was no green glow.

'Cindy?' he called out softly.

There was no answer. Adam stepped out of the bedroom into the hallway. He moved into the living room, checked the kitchen and the den. The house was not that large, he covered it all in less than a minute. He even peeked inside her mother's and brother's bedrooms, on the off-chance she was waiting for him in there. But there was no Cindy.

Adam felt panic. He had to fight to resist it.

Back in her bedroom, he stuck his head inside the closet and turned on the flashlight he had brought. Yet even though the chair had been knocked over, it did not appear as if anything inside the closet had been disturbed. Her clothes were all on their hangers. Her shoes were neatly lined up on top of their respective shoe boxes. Even the hats

Sally had tried on earlier were back in place. The closet, in other words, did not look like the scene of a crime.

Yet Cindy had said the green glow was back.

And now Cindy was gone.

Using his flashlight, Adam found the phone and dialled Watch. As he waited for his friend to answer, Adam reached over and turned on the lamp. The electricity seemed to be working fine. The warm yellow light flooded the bedroom. Watch answered on the second ring. He did not sound like he had been in bed. For all any of them could tell, Watch seemed to live alone, although he usually told people that he lived with his uncle or his grandfather. The relative changed with the account. None of them really liked to pry into Watch's private life.

'Hello?' Watch said.

'This is Adam,' Adam said in a soft voice. 'I'm in Cindy's bedroom. She called me ten minutes ago, said the glow was back. I drove over here as fast as I could on my bike but by the time I got here she was gone.'

'Where did she go?'

'I have no idea. But someone knocked over a chair in her room.' Adam paused. 'I think something's grabbed her.'

'From inside the closet?'

'Yeah, from inside or outside. I don't know what to do. Can you come over here?'

'You sound scared.'

'I am scared,' Adam admitted.

'Sure, I'll come. Call the others as well. This mystery might take everyone's brain to solve.'

Adam paused. He knew how much Watch liked Tira yet he himself did not feel he knew Tira well enough to invite her into the dangerous side of their lives.

'Should I call Tira?' he asked finally.

Watch did not hesitate. 'I'll call her myself. We might need her sensitivity more than anything else.'

'But . . .' Adam began.

'But what?'

'It's the middle of the night. I think she's still recovering from the shock of being possessed for two centuries. Do you want to risk bringing her into this?'

Watch paused. 'Don't you trust her?'

'Sure. Why shouldn't I trust her?'

'Because she was, as you say, possessed only a short time ago.'

'I trust her, Watch, really. We just don't know her that well, that's all.'

'Look, I think she can help us on this one. I want her there. Cindy's safety is all that matters, you know.'

'I know,' Adam muttered.

But for all he knew, Cindy might already be dead.

The gang did not take long to gather. Twenty minutes after Adam called they were all present in Cindy's bedroom. Remarkably, Cindy's mother and brother continued to sleep peacefully in the adjacent rooms. Bryce and Watch examined the closet closely before they stopped to talk. Sally, Adam and Tira stood uneasily nearby. Sally was not joking any more.

Finally the boys were ready to report on the closet.

'There is absolutely nothing unusual about this closet,' Bryce said.

'There is absolutely no sign of what could have produced the green glow,' Watch agreed.

'Who cares about the green glow?' Sally said. 'Where is Cindy?'

'We are assuming the light got her,' Bryce said.

'And did what with her?' Sally asked.

Bryce shrugged. 'Maybe it ate her alive.'

Adam spoke strongly. 'We are operating on the assumption that Cindy is alive. I don't want to hear any talk about anyone being eaten alive.'

Bryce lowered his head. 'I was just stating a possibility. I care about her as much as you guys. I hope she's still alive.'

'Let us assume for a moment that the light took her,' Watch said. 'We have to ask ourselves why the light appeared here, in her closet, before we can even begin to imagine where it took her.'

'It might have been a coincidence that it was her closet,' Sally said. 'Weird stuff happens all over this town.'

'Like I said,' Bryce agreed, 'I can't find anything special about this closet.'

Watch considered. 'Maybe we are looking at this backwards. Maybe it is not the closet that matters here. Maybe it is Cindy herself.'

'What do you mean?' Adam asked.

'I am not sure,' said Watch, turning to Tira. He gestured to her, then to the closet. 'Do you feel anything here that you didn't feel this afternoon?'

Tira momentarily closed her clear blue eyes. When she reopened them she seemed a shade paler. She took a step towards the closet and touched the open door with her palm.

'I feel fear,' she whispered.

Watch stood close. 'Whose fear? Cindy's?'

Tira looked at him, her eyes wide. 'Just fear. This place is soaked in it.'

'How can a place be soaked in fear?' Sally asked.

'I don't know how to explain it,' Tira said. 'It just is.'

Adam stared at their strange new friend. 'Cindy said the green glow seemed to soak into everything in her closet,' he muttered.

'Interesting,' Watch muttered.

'Wait a second,' Sally interrupted. 'Are you guys saying that Cindy's fear created the green glow? If you are then I think you have lost your minds.'

'It may be that her fear did not create the glow,' Watch said. 'But it may have allowed the green glow to come here, to this of all closets.'

'I am not sure if I follow you,' Bryce said.

'It is what I was saying before,' Watch explained. 'We are assuming there is something weird about this closet. It seems a logical assumption. After all, the weird light came from here. But maybe Cindy had a part in that light showing up here, in the middle of the night, and not somewhere else. I remember how Cindy used to say how, at night, the sight of her half-opened closet used to scare her.'

'But that is not unusual,' Sally said. 'Many kids are afraid that something might suddenly come out of their closets and grab them. Many adults have the same fear.'

'You are right,' Watch said. 'And that fact makes what I am going to suggest even more plausible. I suspect that Cindy has been afraid of her dark closet ever since she moved back to Spooksville. What I am suggesting is that that fear built up over time, in this spot, and allowed whatever attacked her an opening into her bedroom.'

Sally shook her head. 'That is a wild theory to propose based on no evidence. Is it not possible that Cindy is just trying to spook us all by going for a long walk in the middle of the night?'

'Cindy was terrified when she called,' Adam said.

'She could have been faking her fear,' Sally said.

'That would have been unlike her.' Watch said.

'Let me see if I understand you right,' Bryce said to Watch. 'You're saying that Cindy's fear of something evil living in her dark closet slowly built up over time and created a rupture in the space-time continuum that allowed a real evil entity to cross over into this dimension and abduct her back to its dimension?'

'Exactly,' Watch said.

'Whatever that means,' Sally muttered.

'It makes sense to me if we start with the idea that it is Cindy that is unique and not the closet,' Watch said.

'Because she is the biggest coward in the group?' Sally asked.

'No,' Watch said. 'We are all afraid of something. It is just that Cindy's fear focused on this particular closet and caused, I believe, the rupture Bryce spoke of.' He paused. 'Tira is sensitive to things we are not. Her senses back up my theory.'

Sally turned to Tira. 'Do you agree with this wild idea?'

Tira nodded solemnly. 'Watch is almost always right.'

Sally sighed. 'I hate hero worship among friends.'

Bryce spoke to Watch. 'But if what you say is true then we need Cindy – and her fear – to reopen this rupture.'

Watch was grim. 'It is possible we will never be able to reopen the rupture.'

Adam spoke up. 'I don't agree. If it is fear that caused whatever it was to invade our world, then we just have to generate that fear again.'

'But we cannot fake our fear,' Watch said. 'It has to be genuine. And I believe it has to have built up over time, like it was in this bedroom.' He added,

'That may be why she only saw the green glow in the dark. It was only in the dark that she felt really afraid.'

'I know a kid who feels afraid just walking to school in the morning,' Sally said.

Adam was interested. 'Who?'

'George Sanders,' Sally said. 'You guys remember him? He's the new kid in town. He helped us fight the Creature in the Teacher – Mr Snakol. George is afraid of his own shadow. If this green glow is out looking for victims in this town, then I bet it has George's address.'

Adam was excited. 'I do remember this George. He was a real coward. Maybe he is someone we can use to reopen the rupture.'

'Even if we are able to get his help,' Watch said. 'We may open a doorway into a place totally different from the one where Cindy is.'

'But that is a chance we have to take,' Adam said. 'We can't just stand here all night and talk and hope Cindy suddenly shows up. We have to take action.'

'But if George is such a coward,' Bryce said, 'how

are we going to talk him into helping us?'

'He will help us even if he doesn't want to help us,' Sally said. 'In fact, it might be better if he doesn't want to help us.'

'I don't understand,' Bryce said.

Sally rubbed her hands together. 'Just leave George to me. I will have him so frightened that he will want to put a padlock on his closet door.'

Five

When Cindy came to, she found herself in a dark forest. She actually awoke lying on her back on the ground, on the grass of a small meadow enclosed by tall shaggy trees. Sitting up, she noticed that the sky glowed with a faint green light. It did not seem to be overcast, but there were no stars, no moon. In the distance she could see the outline of huge shapes that could have been mountains. There was the sound of running water but it was not close. It was not so dark that she could not move around, and yet everything looked slightly blurred. She wondered if it was her own eyesight but when she blinked and rubbed her eyes it made no difference.

She was in a no-man's land.

At least the thing that had grabbed her was nowhere to be seen. She shuddered at the memory of it, although she could not remember it well. Its attack on her had been a blur as well. She vaguely recalled a bulbous body, huge green eyes, grasping hands and a slobbering mouth filled with sharp teeth. It had rushed towards her at incredible speed and then she had blacked out. Or maybe she had screamed and then blacked out. She wondered if anyone had heard her being attacked; if Adam and her other friends were looking for her right now.

But where was she for them to look?

At the rear of her closet?

No, the thing that had grabbed her had definitely emerged from this strange realm. But what it wanted with her she could not imagine. She was just grateful that it had not harmed her.

Cindy stood up and looked around, brushing off her pyjama bottoms.

There was a sound behind her, in the woods.

She whirled and saw a thin, elfish-looking boy. His ears were pointed and his skin glowed with a faint green colour. He wore a simple brown tunic and a grey cloak that reached to his knees. In the leather belt around his waist hung a long silver sword. He stared at her with large green eyes as his right hand rested on the hilt of the blade. Over his shoulder he carried a long bow and a crude bag of arrows. He was slightly taller than her and appeared well-muscled despite his slight frame. His expression was rather intense; he did not look happy to see her.

'You are awake,' he said in a soft clear voice. 'I have been waiting.'

'You speak English,' she said in surprise.

'I speak whatever you speak.'

'What do you mean?'

He let go of his sword and touched the side of his head. 'It comes to me, what to say to you.'

'You mean, you can read my mind?'

'No.'

'Then you knew how to speak English before you met me?'

'No.'

'I don't understand,' Cindy said.

'You are human. Humans are slow to understand.'

Cindy felt mildly insulted. 'What are you?'

'I am Zeta. You are in the realm of Cetine.'

'But how did I get here?'

He paused to look past her. He seemed to frown.

'I can only assume you were brought here by a Shadow,' he said. 'I chanced upon you while you were in its arms.' He paused and touched his sword again. He gestured to the trees on the other side of the small meadow. 'I slew it.'

'Why did you kill it?'

'It was in my way. It would have killed you.'

Cindy grimaced. 'Really?'

He nodded. 'It would have boiled you alive and then eaten your brains. The Shadows love human brains. For them they are a delicacy.'

Cindy felt sick to her stomach. 'Thank you for rescuing me. But where do these Shadows come from?'

'They haunt this part of Cetine. They have always been here.' His voice took on a note of disapproval. 'Most people are wise enough not to enter these lands.'

40

'I didn't plan on coming here at all. I am from Spooksville, I mean Springville. Do you know where that is?'

'Are you from planet Earth?'

'Yes.'

He nodded. 'I know where Earth is.'

'Good. Do you know how I can get back there?'

'You cannot get back. Earth is on the other side of the Curtain.'

'What Curtain?'

He gestured to the weird sky. 'The Curtain of Dreams.'

Cindy began to worry. 'But I have to get back. I have homework to do tomorrow. I have a family, a mother and little brother. I don't belong in this place.'

He turned away. 'That is not my concern.'

'Wait! Where are you going?'

He paused. 'I am returning to Centrae.'

'What is that?'

'The capital of Cetine. It is where Furma lives, the High Lord of all Cetine.'

'Who is this Furma?'

41

'I just told you. Who are you?'

'My name is Cindy Makey.' She offered her hand. She didn't want him to run off and leave her, not with Shadows haunting the woods. Boy, they sounded awful. She hated even having a headache, never mind having someone actually eating her brains. But Zeta just stared at her hand and didn't take it. She added, 'Can I go with you?'

He considered. 'You will slow me down.'

'I am not so slow.' She added, 'You can't just leave me here.'

'Why not?'

'You said it yourself, the woods are full of Shadows. I might be attacked again.'

'That is not my concern.'

'But it has to be your concern. Look, you saved me the first time. Why won't you help me now?'

'I slew the Shadow who captured you because the beast crossed my path. Otherwise I would not have got involved.'

'But you waited nearby for me to wake up?'

'I was merely resting myself.'

'You would have just let it eat my brains?'

'Yes.'

Cindy was annoyed. 'You are not very friendly, you know that?'

'That does not concern me either.'

'What does concern you?'

'Returning to Centrae as swiftly as possible.'

'I need to go to Centrae with you. I need to meet this Furma character.'

'He is not a character. He is High Lord of all Cetine.'

'Yeah, I know that. I heard you the first time. I need to meet with him and see if he knows how to return me to Earth.' She paused. 'I assume he is really wise and all-powerful and stuff like that?'

Zeta hesitated. 'He is wise and powerful.'

'But?' From his tone, it sounded as if Furma might not be that friendly.

'I did not say the word "but".'

'But do you think he would be able to help me?'

'I do not know. I do not care.' Zeta turned to leave, stepping into the trees. 'If you wish to follow me, you may. But I will not slow down for you. You will have to keep up using your own power. And if we are attacked by Shadows, I will defend myself first and you second.'

Cindy scampered to catch up with Zeta. He walked briskly.

'At least you will try to defend me.' She teased, 'I think you must like me a little.'

'I do not care for humans at all.'

'Why not?'

'They look strange. They act strange.'

'Well, where I come from you would look kind of strange, with those pointed ears and all. Have you ever thought of that?'

'No. I do not care what humans think.'

Cindy sighed. 'How far is it to Centrae?'

'By your standards, more than one day's hard hike.'

'Will we stop and rest between here and there?'

'You can stop and rest. But I will not stop.'

'You really would just leave me to be eaten by the Shadows?'

'Yes.'

Cindy shook her head. 'You have a bad attitude, you know that?'

'You said that already. It is not my . . .'

'It is not your concern,' Cindy interrupted.

'Yeah, you said that already.'

Six

At George Sanders's house, the gang gathered outside his bedroom window and knocked stiffly on the glass. The little guy with the big nose and the awkward body took several seconds to answer. He had on red Christmas pyjamas. He even wore a red Santa cap that looked totally ridiculous on top of his bushy eyebrows. He was surprised to see them.

'What are you guys doing here?' he asked.

Sally took the lead. 'We have come to warn you.'

He looked worried. 'Are the aliens back?'

'No,' Sally said. 'It's much worse than that. You remember Cindy Makey?'

'The pretty girl with the blonde hair?'

'She's not that pretty. Anyway, she's been abducted by a horrible monster.'

George put his hand to his mouth. 'That is terrible. Have you called the police?'

'You cannot call the police in this town,' Adam said flatly.

'Why not?' George asked.

'Because they are all cowards that are afraid to leave the police station,' Sally explained. 'Listen, it is probably already too late for Cindy. We're pretty sure the monster has already had her for dinner. But the reason we are here is to try to save your life. You see, this monster is a very special kind of monster. It lives in people's closets.'

George trembled visibly. 'In Cindy's closet?'

Sally leaned closer and spoke in a confidential tone.

'It lives in any kind of closet,' she said. 'It could be in your closet right now. But it is only when you are afraid of it that it can get you. It is your fear of it that opens the doorway through which it can enter into this dimension and grab you. Once it has you nothing can save you. But all you have to do is stay cool and you will be all right.' Sally paused. That's what we came to tell you. But now we have to go.' She turned to leave, and so did the others. George looked panic-stricken.

'Wait!' he cried. 'You can't just leave me. I'm scared.'

Sally paused and shook her head sadly. 'Then it will probably come for you tonight. There is nothing we can do for you. I mean, we tried to warn you but it is hopeless. We're really sorry, George.'

'It was nice knowing you, George,' Watch added.

They all turned to leave again.

'Wait!' George begged. 'You have to stay. You have to protect me.'

Sally stopped. 'But you are the only one who can protect yourself. I already explained that, George. It is only when you get frightened that it can get you.'

'But you shouldn't have told me about it,' George protested. 'I wasn't afraid until you woke me up.'

Sally acted indignant. 'We came here to try to help you. And you don't even have a word of thanks for us. I mean, it is the middle of the night and we all have homework to do tomorrow. We don't have to do this, you know. We're not getting paid.'

George was instantly apologetic. 'I am sorry. I am grateful you stopped by, really, thanks. But you have to stay with me.'

'But if we stay with you,' Watch said, 'then we will not be able to warn other kids in town. They could die while we wait here trying to protect you. Surely you don't want their deaths on your conscience?'

George stuttered. 'No. But . . .'

'And we have to go and talk to Cindy's mother,' Sally interrupted. 'Explain to her that her daughter is gone. It is not a task we take lightly or look forward to.'

George tried to catch his breath. 'Did the monster really kill her?'

'It ate her alive,' Bryce said darkly. 'Ate her brains.'

'And then swallowed her beating heart whole,' Sally added.

George moaned. 'Oh no. That's so terrible.'

'It's a hard world,' Sally said sympathetically.

George struggled. 'But why aren't you guys more upset? She was your friend and all.'

'In this town we have learned not to become too attached to one another,' Adam explained. 'It is better that way. For example, should you be horribly killed in the next few hours, we won't feel too bad.'

'But I will feel bad,' George protested.

'You'll be dead, George,' Watch said. 'You won't feel a thing.' He turned away, and they followed his lead. 'We have done what we can for you. Have a good night.'

'How can I have a good night now?' George wailed. But they didn't stop for him this time. They just kept walking until they were out of his sight, around the side of his house. They stopped in the dark for a hasty conference.

'That guy isn't going to get to sleep tonight,' Sally said.

'You handled him brilliantly,' Watch remarked.

'Thank you,' Sally said. 'Terror is my speciality.'

'Now we have to keep him under observation without letting him see us,' Adam said. 'Where should we hide? Up in the tree in his back yard?'

Watch shook his head. 'That is too far away. If the thing in the closet does appear and grab him, we won't have time to react. We have to be right outside his window.'

'He might see us,' Bryce warned.

'We will have to risk it,' Watch said.

'I don't think it is much of a risk,' Sally said. 'George will be obsessed with his closet from now until the sun comes up. He isn't going to know what's going on outside his window.'

'What are we going to do if the thing does appear?' Tira asked quietly.

Adam frowned. 'That is the question of the night. We are operating on the assumption that we will be able to control this thing. But what if it is stronger than the five of us put together?'

'Then we are in trouble,' Bryce said.

Watch was not so certain. 'There might be some way to render it harmless.'

'Such as?' Sally asked.

'I have no idea,' Watch said.

'You are a big help,' Sally said.

'Whatever happens,' Adam said, 'we cannot just

let it steal George. We have to try to rescue him.'

But Watch shook his head. 'It is more important we enter the realm of the creature, if we are to save Cindy. We can worry about George later.'

'And ourselves?' Sally asked.

But no one had an answer for that question.

They knew what they were attempting was deadly.

Together they quietly crept back into George's back yard and peered through his bedroom window. George had turned on the light and was going through his closet, searching for faults in the wood where a monster might enter. He did this for perhaps half an hour before he finally turned off his light and went back to bed. Like Cindy – they assumed – he had wedged the back of a chair against the closet door knob. But the way he tossed and turned in bed, it didn't look as if he were going to fall asleep any time before the sun rose.

'I wouldn't be surprised if this guy ruptured the back end of the house with his fear,' Sally whispered.

'I feel sorry for him,' Tira said quietly.

'So do I,' Adam admitted.

'Sympathy is a dangerous emotion in this town,' Sally said.

'Shh,' Watch warned. 'You are as worried about Cindy as the rest of us, Sally. Why else would you be here?'

'True,' Sally said. 'But if we do save her, please don't tell her I was worried. I don't want to ruin a perfectly bad relationship.'

They settled down to watch George, the closet, each other. Another hour went by. During that time they began to despair that the green light would show up at all, although George continued to fume and fret in his creaky bed. Certainly they couldn't blame him for not keeping the fear vibes at a high enough level.

Then, finally, a faint green glow shone beneath his closet door.

'There it is!' Sally hissed.

'Stay calm and quiet,' Watch warned. 'The green glow alone does not mean the rupture to the other realm has been created. Remember, Cindy did not see it the first night.'

'George sure sees the light,' Adam said softly. 'Look, he is sitting up in bed. He is shaking with fear.'

Tira sighed. 'I wish we could help him.'

'We can only help Cindy by not helping George,' Bryce reiterated.

They watched as George slowly got out of bed and tried to turn on the light switch. But the power appeared to be dead; the room remained dark. Yet the green glow grew in brilliance as George stood trembling in the middle of his floor. He was now obviously too scared to even run for the door. He knew the monster they had described for him had come for his brains. They could hear him whimpering pitifully.

Carefully, Watch reached up and began to slide open the window.

'We have to be ready to move any second,' he whispered.

'Where are we moving to?' Sally wanted to know.

'We are following the monster straight into its hellish realm,' Bryce said.

Something began to rattle around deep inside the closet.

The chair wedged against the door knob shook.

'I didn't know that was an essential part of the plan,' Sally protested.

'Shh,' Watch warned. 'Stay ready.'

Something banged hard on the closet door.

George let out a choked cry.

The chair shook and fell on its side.

The closet door swung open.

Sickly green light flooded the bedroom.

George turned green. He tried to scream and couldn't.

Something big and horrible rushed out of the closet.

'Let's go!' Watch shouted.

The next few seconds were chaos. The first problem was that they all tried – with the exception of Sally – to climb through the window at the same time. Naturally they all got in each other's way; the window was only so big. Then there was the distraction of the thing grabbing George. It upset their concentration, to say the least.

Yet the monster appeared ill-defined, like thick cloud on moving goo. It was large, much larger than a man, and it was green in colour, the same green as the sickly glow. The thing seemed to have several arms, at least four, and its wicked eyes shone with a fiery light. Yet it seemed to float towards George, rather than walk. They could not be sure it had legs. Still, it moved very fast. Before even one of them could get all the way through the window, it had a hold on George.

The poor guy fainted in its arms.

'Stop!' Adam cried as he stood upright in the room. Watch was at his side in a moment. Tira and Bryce were still bumping into each other in the window. Sally could have been outside doing her nails.

'Grab it!' Watch yelled.

'Where?' Adam shouted back.

'Anywhere!' Watch said.

The thing in the closet already had a firm hold on George. It had swept him off his feet and was turning back in the direction of the closet. For that reason, Adam and Watch both ended up jumping on the creature's back. It was solid enough; it felt them and they certainly felt it. Adam caught a glimpse of a wide angry mouth filled with dripping teeth. Then the thing threw back its shoulder and he went flying towards the far side of the room. Luckily he landed on George's bed. Nevertheless, for a moment, Adam was stunned. He watched in a daze as Sally finally came through the window and kicked the monster in the butt. It was a good thing. The monster was in the middle of trying to take a bite out of Watch's head.

'Take that, you ugly slime!' Sally yelled as she struck the creature. Her blow seemed to hurt it. The monster dropped Watch – but not George – and tried to grab Sally. But now Bryce came to her aid. From somewhere he had found a baseball bat. As the monster bent to snatch Sally, Bryce smacked it over the head as hard as he could. The blow did real damage. The creature staggered back and even its hold on George began to slip. The unconscious boy dropped to the floor. Clearly the creature was not used to so much resistance. Turning, it clawed its way towards the closet, and the wide green opening at the back.

Adam jumped up off the bed and shouted to the others.

'Don't let it get away! Go after it!'

Adam was the first to follow his own advice. He chased the creature into the closet, straight into the brilliant green glow. Watch and Sally were at his heels. Bryce and Tira tried to follow as well, but before they could reach the rear of the closet the rupture into the other dimension closed.

Leaving them panting in the dark with nowhere to go.

Bryce and Tira stood dazed.

George moaned and moved on the floor.

'They're gone,' Tira whispered.

It was true, there were only three of them in the room now.

Bryce nodded grimly. 'But where?' he said.

Seven

Cindy was already exhausted, following Zeta. The guy walked as fast uphill as he did downhill, and there were many hills in this strange land of Cetine. Overhead the dim sky did not change; it continued to shimmer with its faint green glow, painting the entire landscape in eerie tones. It was such a peculiar sky. Cindy remembered how Zeta had gestured to it when he had spoken about the Curtain of Dreams. Sometimes she felt as if she could reach up and touch it.

They stepped over a narrow stream.

The water gurgled in the night. Zeta paused.

'You may stop and have a quick drink,' he said stiffly.

Cindy stopped and knelt beside the stream.

'Is this water good?' she asked.

'Water is water in Cetine. It is all good.'

'Why don't you have a drink then?'

'I am not thirsty.'

'But we have been walking for hours.'

'Humans are frail. They get tired and thirsty much more easily than the people of Cetine.'

Cindy brushed her blonde hair aside and leaned over and had a sip of the clear liquid. It was warmer than she expected, and had a faint sweet taste that reminded her of honey. On the whole it was delicious. She felt greatly refreshed as the liquid seemed to spread through her body.

'What is it that you have against humans?' she asked. It was only as she looked up at him that she noticed he had only four toes on each foot. One big one and three little ones. For that matter, he only had four fingers on each hand. It must be hard, she thought, to count in this place.

'I have nothing against humans. I am merely stating facts.'

'Have you ever met a human before? Before you met me?'

Zeta hesitated. 'Briefly.'

'Where are they now? In Centrae?'

'No.'

'Where?' she persisted.

'In the bellies of the Shadows.'

Cindy flinched. 'You saw these people get eaten?'

'Yes.'

'Did you do anything to help them?'

'No.'

Cindy was angry. 'Why not? And don't tell me it was not your concern.'

Zeta paused. 'There were too many Shadows. I was not able to help.'

There was a faint note of regret in his voice. Cindy stood up.

'Why does the Most High Furma allow these creatures to wander loose?' she asked.

Zeta gave her a sharp look, as if to snap at her. But then he turned away.

'I do not know,' he said quietly.

'Why are you hiking in this land? If it is so dangerous?'

'You ask many questions, Cindy Makey.'

'They are good questions. Why are you here?'

Zeta was thoughtful. 'This land is called the Forbidden Territories. Here I am studying the Shadows. I am trying to learn their ways.'

'Why?'

'To report to Furma.'

'So he sent you here personally?'

'No. I came of my own free will.'

'What do you hope to gain by reporting to Furma about the Shadows?'

'I wish to persuade him that they must be contained. I want him to send his army against the creatures.'

'Forgive me for saying this, but you don't look any older than myself. How do you happen to know Furma?'

'He is my uncle.'

'You are the King's nephew?'

'Yes.'

Cindy smiled. 'I'm impressed.'

'I did not tell you to impress you.'

'Are you sure? Are you sure you don't like human girls just a little bit?'

Zeta lowered his head. 'Have you finished your drink, Cindy Makey?'

'Just call me Cindy?'

'Have you finished?' he asked.

'Yes. But do you have to walk so fast? I am getting tired.'

'We must reach Centrae by nightfall.'

'What are you talking about? It is already night.'

Zeta shook his head. 'This is daytime in my realm. When night comes it is impossible to see anything. It is then that the Shadows are most dangerous.'

Cindy shuddered. 'Are there really that many in this area?'

Zeta paused to sniff the air. 'They are everywhere in these parts. We must keep moving.' He turned to walk away from the stream, up another exhausting hill. Cindy hurried to follow.

'Can I keep talking?' she asked.

'It seems there is no stopping you from talking. Please speak quietly.'

'You said please, Zeta. I am impressed.'

'I tell you, I am not trying to impress you.'

'I believe you,' she said. 'When you spoke of the Shadows being contained, did you mean that their numbers have grown?'

'It would seem so.'

'What are they like. I mean, are they like big animals?'

'No.'

'Could you please elaborate?' she asked.

'You were attacked by one. You must have seen it.'

'Not very well. I think I fainted.'

Zeta sneered faintly. 'A typical human response to danger.'

'Where do they come from? Do they have little babies like other wild animals?'

Zeta paused, and then spoke seriously.

'It is a mystery. Many of the wise men and women of Centrae debate this point.' He paused and seemed to shudder. 'Some believe they come from the remains of our unconsumed fears.'

Cindy frowned. 'What do you mean? Do your people create them?'

Zeta shook his head and searched the forest.

'It is not wise to talk about such things in these parts,' he said.

Cindy hesitated. 'OK. I was just curious, that's all.'

'Curiosity about the Shadows is never healthy.'

'For a human?'

'For anyone,' he said darkly.

'What is Furma like?'

'He is the High Lord of all Cetine.'

'Yeah, I heard you the first time. But what is he like as a person?'

'Are you asking if he likes humans?'

'Yeah. Does he?'

'No.'

Cindy frowned. 'Oh. Do you think he will want to help me?'

'No.'

'Then why are you taking me to him?'

'You insisted on seeing him. I am not taking you anywhere.'

'But do you think he really does know how I can get back to Earth?'

Zeta was unsure. 'Furma knows many things. But most of what he knows, he does not speak of.'

There was a peculiar note in Zeta's voice when he spoke of Furma.

'You do not get along with your uncle, do you?'

'I never call him my uncle. He is the High Lord of all Cetine.'

'Do you get along with him?' Cindy persisted.

Zeta paused. 'I do not understand his mind. I do not understand why he does not declare war on the Shadows. I worry that . . .' Zeta did not finish.

'What do you worry?' Cindy asked.

But Zeta refused to answer.

They continued to hike. If anything, Zeta increased his pace. Cindy found herself growing hot and sweaty. There was not a clear path through the forest. She had to keep her arms out in front of her to keep branches from slapping her in the face. They passed numerous streams and Zeta let her pause to drink occasionally, but he did not really let her rest. The passing day concerned him greatly. Cindy could not imagine that it could get much darker, yet the sheer blackness that he spoke of drove her on.

They were cresting a particularly tall hill when Zeta suddenly stopped. He sniffed the air as Cindy came close to his side.

'What is it?' she whispered.

'They're close,' he said quietly.

'The Shadows?'

'Yes. They are tracking us.'

Cindy was terrified. 'Are you sure?'

'Yes.' He glanced around. 'We are exposed on this hill. We must get down.' He gestured to a narrow river at the centre of the gorge in front of them. 'There is a cave not far upstream. If we can make it that far, we will have a chance of defending ourselves. It is our only hope.'

'How many Shadows follow us? Do you know?'

Zeta gripped the hilt of his silver sword. 'At least a dozen.'

Cindy felt she might faint again. 'How can we stop them? What are they afraid of?'

'Nothing,' Zeta said.

They ran down the hill, as best they could. But

the foliage was so thick that Cindy stumbled several times. To her immense relief, Zeta did not leave her behind. Each time he halted to pick her up. But behind them was the sound of many scurrying feet. Cindy could hear the creatures but could not see them, which just intensified her fear.

Finally they reached the river.

Cindy was out of breath but she turned to run upstream.

Zeta stopped her.

'It is too late,' he said.

'What do you mean?' she gasped.

He sniffed the air. 'They know of the cave. They have cut off our escape.'

Cindy was a mass of nerves. 'But what are we going to do?'

Zeta upholstered his bow. 'We must make a stand. We must kill as many as possible before they overwhelm us.'

'But I don't want to be overwhelmed. I want to live.'

Zeta withdrew a knife from his back pocket and

handed it to her. At last there was compassion in his eyes.

'You must fight,' he said. 'But if the fight goes poorly, then you must not let them take you alive.'

Cindy pushed away the knife in horror.

'No,' she gasped. 'I can't do that. I can't take my own life.'

He shoved the knife back at her.

'And you can't let them take you,' he said gently. 'You do not understand what they would do to you. Death is better.'

Cindy shook her head desperately.

The sounds in the dark woods were getting closer.

Yet an unlooked for wave of courage flowed through her.

'Death is never better,' she said, finally taking the knife and tightening her grip on the handle. 'I will fight but I will not surrender. To the Shadows or to death.'

Zeta for once smiled. 'You are brave for a human, Cindy.'

But her brave words did not serve her in the next few minutes.

Cindy saw a green mass off to her left. Zeta pivoted and let fly an arrow. The tiny spear flew through the forest. The creature let out a gut-piercing cry and toppled. But two more creatures appeared off to their left. They were hideous; their eyes seemed to burn with flame and hunger. Zeta managed to get off another arrow, and kill another one of them. But the third one was on them before he could fit another arrow in his bow. Zeta managed to draw his sword but the Shadow jumped him. Everything was happening so fast. Cindy raised her knife to try to stab it in the back, but then she sensed a huge shape at her back. She whirled to see a thick arm swinging towards her face.

Then she felt a hard blow.

It almost felt as if her head exploded.

Then there was darkness.

Eight

For Sally, Watch, and Adam it was as if they fell from the sky. Toppled from darkness into night. Yet when they hit the ground they didn't actually hurt themselves. They were on their feet in a moment. The green beast they had pursued through the rear of the closet stood in front of them. Sally quickly picked up a rock and threw it at the thing, hitting him on the head. The creature had had enough of them. With a growl, it turned and fled into the forest.

What forest?

Where were they?

The three of them looked at each other in wonder.

'We made it,' Adam gushed.

Sally was gloomy, as gloomy as the dark forest.

'Somehow I don't feel like celebrating just yet,' she said.

Watch studied the environment, particularly the sky. It seemed to hang directly above their heads, and shone with a faint green light.

'We are definitely in another dimension,' he said. 'I hope it is the same one Cindy vanished into.'

'I hope one of those monsters didn't eat her the moment she arrived,' Sally added.

'We agreed not to talk about Cindy being dead,' Adam said.

Watch studied the ground. He pointed.

'There are two sets of footprints here,' he said. 'One of them looks like it could belong to Cindy.'

Adam knelt beside the impressions in the soft ground.

'One set of footprints belongs to a four-toed person,' he said.

Watch crouched beside him and nodded. 'They could not have been from earth.'

'Could the prints be from one of the monsters?' Sally asked.

'No,' Watch said leaning over the prints and pushing his thick glasses back on his nose. 'This person was too much like a human.' He paused and searched around. The prints led off to their right. Because the ground was largely soft mud and grass, it seemed it would be no problem to follow them. 'It is possible Cindy ran into help when she arrived here.'

'I hope she did,' Adam said with feeling.

'That would be just like Cindy to take advantage of the natives,' Sally said.

Watch stood up. 'We must follow her.' He drew out a flashlight from his back pocket and turned it on. The white beam pierced the surrounding gloom. 'I'm glad I brought this with me.' He glanced at the strange sky. 'I think it's getting darker.'

Adam also stood up. 'I wonder how far ahead of us she is?'

'Assuming time works parallel to time in our dimension,' Watch said, 'she's got to be at least two hours in front of us.'

Sally studied the footprints. 'One thing's for sure, she doesn't have shoes on.'

'She probably just has her pyjamas on,' Adam said.

'I bet the native boys like that,' Sally remarked.

'Aren't you relieved that she might still be alive?' Adam demanded.

'I will be relieved when we are all home and in bed,' Sally said. 'You guys were clever enough to get us here. Wherever here is. But how are we supposed to get back?'

Watch clutched the flashlight. 'We'll have to worry about that later.'

'Famous last words,' Sally muttered.

They started off in the direction the prints led. From the length of the strides, it looked as if Cindy and her partner were walking at a fast clip. Watch commented on that fact.

'It's possible Cindy's guide was anxious to get her out of this place,' he said. 'That might mean there are a lot of those creatures around.'

'Let's hope they are afraid of your flashlight,' Adam said.

'I wouldn't count on that,' Sally said. 'Adam, why didn't you bring your laser pistol?'

'Don't you remember?' Adam said. 'The witch, Ann Templeton, took it on Halloween night. I don't have it any more.'

'You need to get that thing back,' Sally said.

'Shh,' Watch warned. 'It might be wise not to attract attention to ourselves. We should talk quietly or not at all.'

'I have to talk a little,' Sally said. 'Talking for me is like breathing for most people. I will explode if I can't talk. I even have to talk in my sleep.'

'Then whisper,' Watch said firmly.

They hiked for seemingly ever. Over the next few hours, overhead, the green glow dimmed further and then the sky eventually turned black. Without Watch's flashlight they would have been stuck in one spot. Now they just hoped the batteries held up, even though Watch said he had changed them not long ago.

'But I put cheap batteries in the flashlight,' Watch admitted.

'There should be a rule against buying cheap

batteries in Spooksville,' Sally said. 'We are always ending up in dark and dangerous places.'

Adam breathed hard as they ploughed up still another hill.

'These two really covered some ground,' he said.

Watch nodded. 'I am convinced her guide was trying to reach a certain place before night fell.' He paused. They could hear water in front of them, and below them. They had already passed several streams but this sounded like a full-blown river. 'Do you guys hear that?' Watch asked.

'Of course,' Adam said. 'It sounds like water.'

'No,' said Watch, going still. 'There is something in the woods, near us.' He turned off the light. The absolute darkness was suffocating.

'Turn that back on!' Sally hissed.

'Shh,' Watch warned. 'We cannot necessarily see them with the light on but they can definitely see us. I think it is better to play it safe.'

'Somehow I don't feel very safe at the moment,' Sally said.

'Listen,' Watch said softly. 'The sound is coming closer.'

'Turn on the light,' Sally said desperately. 'It might be one of those monsters. The light might scare it away.'

'But you just said we couldn't count on that,' Adam said.

'I've changed my mind!' Sally croaked.

'Be still,' Watch advised in the perfect blackness. 'I don't think it is one of the creatures. Those sound like human feet.'

'Human feet with four toes or with five toes?' Sally asked anxiously. 'I would prefer five toes.'

'Should we call out to it?' Adam asked.

'No,' Watch said, 'it already knows where we are. It is moving our way.'

'Maybe we should scream,' Sally said through chattering teeth. The tension was unbearable.

'It might be Cindy,' Adam suggested hopefully.

'If it is then she has learned to see in the dark in the last few hours,' Watch said.

They waited. They sweated. Their hearts beat loudly.

The sound – it was really faint – drew closer and closer.

Finally they heard a voice in the blackness.

'Do you three know Cindy Makey?' it asked.

Adam spoke cautiously. 'Yes. We are her friends. Who are you?'

'My name is Zeta. I met Cindy several of your hours ago. I have been travelling with her.'

'Where is she?' Watch asked. 'Is she with you?'

Zeta hesitated. 'No. She has been captured by the Shadows.'

'The Shadows?' Sally said. 'Are they those horrible slimy green monsters?'

Again Zeta paused. 'Yes. They are horrible. Cindy is in extreme danger. I have been circling around the Shadows' camp. I was going to try to rescue her.'

'How did you let her get captured in the first place?' Sally demanded.

There was a note of sorrow in Zeta's voice.

'We were attacked at the river below. There were too many of them. I had to fight off half-a-dozen. When I turned to get Cindy, she had already been dragged off.'

'A likely story,' Sally said.

'Sally,' Adam warned. 'Don't be rude.'

'Don't be rude?' Sally complained 'This weird guy with four toes shows up in the middle of the night and says he was travelling with our friend but now she has been captured by the Shadow creatures, and you just decide to trust him. We don't know this guy from Adam . . . I mean, from anybody. He could be working with the Shadows.'

'I am not in league with them,' Zeta said firmly. 'They are my sworn enemies. If you do not want to help me try to rescue Cindy, then that is up to you. I will try anyway.'

'Why?' Watch asked, curious. 'You just met Cindy. Why risk your life for her?'

For the third time Zeta paused.

'She is my concern,' he said finally. 'She is my friend.'

'How can we help you?' Adam asked.

'A moment ago you carried a powerful light in your hand,' Zeta said. 'Is this light at your command? Can you bring it at will?'

'Yes,' Watch said.

'That is good,' Zeta said. 'We can use that light to startle the Shadows. If we can scare them for even a few moments, then I should be able to slip into their camp and set Cindy free.'

'Have they tied her up?' Adam asked grimly.

'Yes. They have built a huge fire close to here. They are preparing to eat her alive.'

'I knew it,' Sally muttered.

'Can we slip into the camp with you?' Adam asked. 'Can we be of more direct help?'

'No. Humans move too slowly. The Shadows would be all over you in a moment.' Zeta paused. 'I want you to follow me by holding on to my hand. Save your light for now. I will tell you when to command it to shine.'

'I don't know about this,' Sally said. 'How do we know you are not leading us to our deaths?'

'I can prove nothing to you right now,' Zeta said. 'You can remain here or follow me. The choice is yours.'

'I want to follow this guy,' Adam said.

'Me too,' Watch said decisively.

'Great,' Sally complained. 'We haven't even seen

82

the guy's face and we're going to visit a bunch of Shadows with him.'

Zeta spoke carefully. 'What is your name, female?'

'Sarah Wilcox. Why?'

'You are different from Cindy Makey.'

'Are you trying to insult me?'

'I am merely stating a fact,' Zeta said.

Adam took Zeta's hand, Watch took Adam's, and Sally took Watch's. In a chain of four they moved through the black woods. Zeta did not like the way they moved. Several times he told them to be quieter. Indeed, he ordered Sally to keep her mouth shut, not that it did much good. Zeta clearly thought Sally must be from a different dimension from the rest of them. She kept muttering about cannibals and other such things.

They saw a yellow glow up ahead.

In the faint light they caught a glimpse of Zeta's profile.

'This guy has pointed ears,' Sally complained.

Zeta gestured for quiet. It was amazing he knew the gesture.

'We are near the Shadows' camp,' he said. 'Now I must circle around to the right. You who carry the light must creep straight towards their fire. Settle in the trees not far from the burning wood. You will hear a whistle sound. It would sound like a bird sound. That is my signal. At that moment command your light to shine on the faces of the Shadows. It should scare them for a short time. During that time I will be able to free Cindy.'

'Then the Shadows will come after us,' Sally said.

'That is a possibility,' Zeta agreed. 'But I can think of no other way to save Cindy from a horrible death.'

'Not that you would mind seeing me die horribly,' Sally said.

'Zeta,' Adam said. 'You have a sword as well as a bow and arrows. Can we borrow one of the weapons? While Watch is shining the light, I might be able to hold off any charging Shadows.'

Zeta offered his sword to Adam. 'I have a knife I gave to Cindy – which she dropped – that I can use to untie her bonds. But to kill a Shadow you must stab them in the heart. It is the only place where they are vulnerable.'

'What if you cut off their heads?' Adam asked.

'It will only slow them down,' Zeta said. 'They are not like normal living creatures.'

'I should say not,' Sally remarked.

Zeta looked at them. 'It is not the custom in my world to wish people good luck, but I understand from Cindy that you have such superstitions. So I wish you good luck now, all of you.'

'Good luck to you too,' Sally said.

They all stared at her in amazement.

Zeta vanished into the woods. Watch and Adam crept slowly forwards. Sally tagged along behind them.

'You don't have to come with us,' Adam told her.

'Like I would enjoy waiting in the pitch dark for you to return,' Sally said.

They drew closer to the bonfire.

They could hear the Shadows hooting and hollering.

'Now I wish you still had your laser pistol,' Watch said.

'I will beg the witch for it the next time I see her,' Adam said.

They saw the Shadows – there must have been ten of them. They danced around their fire, the slobber flowing from their mouths. It seemed they were waiting for the big black pot in the centre of the fire to start boiling. Off to the far side lay Cindy. She was tied up, bound to a tree. It was even possible she was unconscious. Certainly she was not moving. The three of them stared in horror.

'I hope she is still alive,' Sally whispered.

'Zeta says that she is,' Adam said quickly.

'This fire is pretty bright,' Watch said. 'I don't know if this flashlight will make that much impression on these creatures.'

'But it gives off a white light,' Adam said, lifting the sword. It was heavier than it looked. 'They have probably never seen anything like it.'

'Let's hope not,' Watch said.

They heard a faint whistle sound.

The Shadows ignored it.

The three humans stared at each other.

Then Watch jumped to his feet and shone the light in the faces of the Shadows.

Sally also jumped up and began to howl like a wolf.

Watch and Adam looked at her as if she had lost her mind.

'They might think I am a werewolf,' she paused long enough to say.

The flashlight, or maybe the howling, scared the Shadows. For a moment there was panic around the fire. Several of the creatures ran into each other, bumping their comrades into the flames. A couple actually caught fire and began to howl worse than Sally. On the far side of the clearing, they saw Zeta kneel beside Cindy and begin to cut into her bonds.

Then the Shadows suddenly stopped fussing and stared in the direction of the flashlight. Even the ones who were on fire managed to put themselves out and regain their nerve. The three humans began to worry.

'Now we're in trouble,' Sally muttered.

Slowly the Shadows seemed to come back to life. They moved towards them.

'Sally,' Watch said, 'do you have your Bic lighter with you?'

'Sure,' Sally said. 'What do you want me to do with it? Light them an after dinner cigar?'

'Throw it into the fire,' Watch said. 'The flames will cause it to explode. That might scare them more than the flashlight.'

Sally whipped out her lighter. 'I hope you're right. You know this thing cost me fifty cents.'

Sally threw the lighter into the fire.

Zeta had already freed Cindy.

He disappeared into the woods, carrying her in his arms.

It took a moment but then the lighter exploded.

The sound was loud. It seemed to startle the Shadows.

Watch turned off the flashlight and whirled.

'Let's get out of here,' he called.

The others chased after him.

'Where are we going?' Adam asked.

'Back to the river,' Watch said. 'Remember Zeta said he would meet us there.'

'But what if the Shadows follow us?' Sally asked.

'Then everything you have always worried about and complained about all your life will happen to us all at once and then you will never have to worry or complain again because you will be dead,' Watch said.

'Oh,' Sally said.

Yet, strangely, the Shadows did not follow them.

Soon they were reunited with Zeta and Cindy. Zeta led them all across the river, to a nearby cave where he thought they would be safe for the night.

Cindy was all right. She was overjoyed to see them.

'I can't believe you guys came after me,' she exclaimed, giving each of them a big hug, even Sally. 'How did you do it?'

'You have George Sanders to thank,' Sally said.

Cindy was puzzled. 'George?'

'It's a long story,' Adam said.

Nine

The next morning broke dark and gloomy. The gang woke to find Zeta sitting guard at the cave entrance.

'Did you sleep at all?' Cindy asked, worried.

Zeta smiled faintly. He seemed fond of Cindy.

'I do not need as much rest as you humans,' he said.

Cindy laughed and punched his arm. 'Don't start that stuff again. You are finally learning some manners.'

Watch peered outside the cave. 'Your days are dark. Is there any danger of the Shadows attacking at this time?'

'Yes,' Zeta said. 'But this is their slow time. They usually rest right after night. We would be wise to hurry towards Centrae while we have the chance.'

'What are we going to do there?' Sally grumbled. She did not like sleeping on hard rock floors, particularly without her favourite pillow.

'Zeta is going to get us a meeting with Furma, the High Lord of all Cetine,' Cindy said. 'Furma is Zeta's uncle. Zeta is royalty.'

'And what is this Fur guy going to do for us?' Sally asked.

Cindy glanced doubtfully at Zeta.

'We're hoping he can help us get back to Earth,' Cindy said without conviction. The others noticed her lack of enthusiasm, and the fact that Zeta lowered his head as she spoke.

'Can he help us?' Adam asked Zeta.

Zeta glanced up. 'First he has to want to help you. To be honest, I am not sure if that is the case. He has never been fond of humans.'

'So others from Earth have been to this dimension?' Watch asked.

'Yes,' Zeta said.

'How did they get here?' Adam asked.

Zeta shrugged. 'I assume the Shadows kidnapped them from your world. Is that not how you got here?'

'That's how I got here,' Cindy said.

'We used a similar route,' Watch admitted. 'But what I want to know is, what is your uncle's relationship to the Shadows? Cindy said during the night that you told her your uncle was reluctant to move against them.'

'That is true and I do not understand why,' Zeta admitted.

'Is it possible he is in league with them?' Watch persisted.

'No,' Zeta said firmly. 'You saw them. The Shadows are the enemies of all living beings.'

'But does your uncle have other political enemies?' Watch asked. 'You call him the High Lord and all that, but are there other factions in the land?'

Zeta was quiet for a moment. The questions disturbed him.

'There is a land beyond Cetine called Gilbrare,'

Zeta said finally. 'It is not as large as Cetine but its people are powerful. Lately we have battled with them. Not a full-scale war, but repeated skirmishes.'

'What is the fighting about?' Adam asked.

'They refuse to recognise my uncle as King,' Zeta said. 'They refuse to pay their rightful share of taxes.'

'I can understand that,' Sally muttered.

'If Cetine were to have a full-scale war with Gilbrare, is it possible it could lose?' Watch asked.

Zeta hesitated. 'Yes.'

Watch glanced at Adam, who seemed concerned by these remarks.

'It is possible your uncle is seeking an alliance with the Shadows?' Watch asked carefully. But Zeta shook his head vigorously.

'Why would he go into league with those monsters?' he demanded.

'Why doesn't he push to get rid of those monsters?' Watch asked. 'Desperate people often do desperate things. To me it sounds as if your uncle is cornered. Cindy said you told her he didn't even want you travelling in this area.'

'He was concerned about my safety,' Zeta said.

Adam sighed. 'All these arguments are of no use. Let us return to Centrae now and see what we can learn.'

'Yeah,' Sally said. 'I don't care about local politics. I just want to get home.'

Zeta put his sword back in his belt. 'We will travel swiftly.'

'And he means it,' Cindy said.

Zeta led them out of the cave and back into the forest. For two hours they walked up and down a series of hills like those of the previous day. It did not take long for the gang to feel tired – Zeta walked so fast. But eventually they reached a wide path and the way flattened. Finally, far in the distance, they glimpsed a huge stone city. Zeta paused and pointed.

'There is Centrae,' he said.

'How long till we get there?' Adam asked.

'At this speed, eight hours,' Zeta said. 'But we should be there before night falls. Our days are longer than Earth's.'

'How do you know so much about Earth?' Watch asked.

'There are stories about it in the old books,' Zeta said. 'We know it lies beyond the Curtain of Dreams.'

'What's that?' Watch asked.

'The border of our world, of course,' Zeta said, surprised at the question. He seemed to think they should know what he meant.

They set off once more, at a brisk pace. Perhaps two hours had passed when they noticed a column of horse-drawn wagons approaching them on the path. Zeta stared at them for a long time before speaking. The front one carried a bright green and red flag. The wagons had caused a huge dust cloud to rise. It followed the column like a dark cloud.

'That is Duke Lester's flag,' Zeta said finally. 'I wonder what his people are doing out here.'

'Is he a friend of your uncle?' Cindy asked.

Zeta nodded. 'They are close friends. Duke Lester is one of the few people he trusts completely.'

'And he has sent him to look for you,' Watch remarked.

'Are you suggesting that this Duke might be a threat?' Adam asked.

'I am suggesting that something funny is going on in this area,' Watch said.

'You just got here,' Zeta protested. 'What do you know?'

'For one thing I know that the Shadows let us go last night,' Watch said.

'That is nonsense,' Cindy said. 'They were ready to eat me alive.'

'You, perhaps,' Watch said. 'But I don't think they intended to harm Zeta.'

Zeta was bitter. 'You were not there when I was attacked. I had to fight for my life.'

'But when has anyone ever escaped from so many Shadows?' Watch asked.

Zeta was annoyed. 'You are saying my uncle told them to spare me?'

Watch shrugged. 'Perhaps. Let us talk to this Duke. I am sure he has many interesting things to tell us.'

But they did not need to talk to the Duke Lester. Even as his caravan drew near, they saw that several of the wagons were manned by Shadows. The monsters were actually driving the horses on. Zeta stared in shock and dismay.

'This cannot be happening,' he said.

Duke Lester reached them not long after. A tall man with pointed ears and a stunning red robe, he wore a crystal medallion round his neck. He stood up in the front cart and stepped forward to meet them. He did not seem pleased to see that Zeta had friends with him. He wanted to know who they were.

'I want to know how all these guys know English,' Sally muttered.

'I think they pick it up from our brains,' Cindy muttered back. 'Or else I think we just hear their language as English. Remember, this is a supernatural place.'

Sally scowled at the nearby Shadows. 'I still think those monsters want to eat our brains.'

Zeta bowed slightly at the Duke's question.

'These are humans from earth,' Zeta explained. 'I met them in the Forbidden Territories, and helped them escape the clutches of the Shadows.'

He glanced at the Shadows on the wagons and added, 'But I see I have not helped them far enough from this land.'

The Duke raised his hand. 'You are not to talk about what you have seen here today. That is a command from your uncle.'

Zeta was disturbed. 'Am I to keep silent about an alliance with these monsters? This partnership goes beyond reason. The people must know about it. You know these creatures would eat us alive if they could.'

The Duke smiled thinly. 'But they cannot at the moment. For the time being they are on our side in our war with Gilbrare. That is all that matters – that they can protect your uncle from being toppled from his throne.'

'And when the war is over?' Zeta demanded. 'What will the Shadows do then? What will they want for a reward? How many of us will they want to eat?'

The Duke cut him off with a sharp gesture. 'You and your friends are to climb aboard the rear wagon. You will be escorted back to Centrae. There

99

you will await the King's judgment.'

'But my friends and I have done nothing wrong,'
Zeta said.

The Duke raised an angry eyebrow. 'Oh? You
chose to spy in the Forbidden Territories when you
were told not to.'

'I came here to collect information to aid my
uncle,' Zeta said.

'And you have learned more than you should
have,' the duke said, turning away. 'Get in the last
wagon. There will be no more discussion on this
point.'

The Duke strode away. His guards stepped forward.

They carried long swords and looked serious.

The last wagon was manned by Shadows.

They slobbered hungrily as they waited.

Zeta turned to Watch. 'It seems everything you
said is true. How did you know?'

'I understand rulers,' Watch said. 'For most of
them, sadly, nothing is more important to them
than staying in power. It is the same in our world.
That is all I had to know to figure out what was
going on here.'

Adam patted Zeta on the back. 'I am sorry about all this. We seem to have landed here at the wrong time.'

'Yeah,' Sally grumbled. 'And it looks like we're never going to get out of here."

Ten

Later that same day they found themselves in a cold and dark stone prison far beneath the main palace. At least that was where Zeta thought they had been taken. After the Duke's guards had escorted them into the last wagon, they had been locked away from all sights and sounds. They had actually been blindfolded when the wagon stopped. The blinds had only been removed when they were shoved roughly into the prison.

At least they were together, and there seemed to be no Shadows in the immediate area. The gang sat on the stone floor and watched while Zeta anxiously paced. Their only light was from a burning torch placed high in the corner. They had been in the prison for over an hour and were getting hungry and thirsty.

'I don't suppose you can call for room service in this place,' Sally said.

'I do not understand why my uncle has not sent for us,' Zeta said. 'He has to meet with me soon. I have to explain to him that this is all wrong.'

'Furma will not talk to you today,' Watch said. 'He may not talk to you until the war is over.'

Zeta stopped in his tracks. 'That is impossible.'

'Watch is right,' Adam said. 'The King cannot allow his secret to be known until the war is in full swing and your people are winning. Then and only then will he be able to justify an alliance with the Shadows.'

Zeta looked weary. 'You humans have a skill for bluntness.'

'It comes from living in Spooksville,' Sally said.

Zeta finally sat down. 'This Spooksville you speak of – is it a great kingdom on Earth?'

'It is just a small haunted coastal town,' Sally said.

'But it is home nevertheless,' Cindy said. 'We feel bad about what is going on here, really Zeta, but we do have to get back to our families. They will be worrying about us.'

'I am the one who feels bad,' Zeta said. 'I do not know how to return you to your home. But one thing's for sure – my uncle will do nothing to help you now.'

'I am still curious about this expression you use,' Watch said to Zeta. 'The Curtain of Dreams. You said it encloses your world. What did you mean by that exactly?'

Zeta gestured above. 'It is just there. It covers everything.'

Watch leaned forward. 'You gesture upwards. By *it* do you mean the sky?'

'Yes, of course. The Curtain of Dreams. It separates our world from others. Is it not the same in your world?'

'Not exactly,' said Watch before turning to Adam and Sally. 'Do you remember that falling sensation right after we chased the Shadow through the rear of George's closet?'

'Yeah,' Adam said. 'I thought we were going to hurt ourselves when we landed.'

Watch nodded 'Each of us fell as if we'd landed. And maybe we had.'

'What are you saying?' Sally asked. 'That we fell out of the sky when we came here?'

Watch paused. 'Yes.'

Sally laughed. 'That is the stupidest thing I ever heard.

'I wonder,' Watch said. 'I have studied the sky here. This may sound odd but it does not seem that far away.'

'But the sky is the sky,' Sally protested. 'It is not in one fixed place.'

'In our world perhaps,' Watch said. 'But here might be a different story. Zeta?'

'Of course the sky is like a curtain,' Zeta said, puzzled. 'It is fixed. How could it be otherwise?'

Adam sat up. 'Watch, are you saying that earth is just on the other side of this curtain? That if we can get up to the sky we might be able to get back home?'

'Yes,' Watch said. 'On the condition that we can

reach the sky and somehow manage to open it. Zeta, tell me, are there any high mountains in this land that reach up to the curtain?'

'Of course,' Zeta said. 'The Curtain of Dreams rests on several of the highest mountains. There is a peak not far from here that touches the sky.'

'This place is too weird,' Sally muttered.

'Could you take us to that peak?' Watch asked.

Zeta nodded. 'When my uncle lets us out of here we will go there immediately. On horseback it is only a short ride from here. A few of your hours, no more.'

'I don't think we will be going there today,' Adam said grimly.

Just then they heard a knock on their prison door.

Zeta jumped up and hurried to the door. There was a small square of metal bars on the door through which he could see the outside. A small figure with a burning torch seemed to be standing in the stone hallway. Zeta recognised her.

'Clere!' he exclaimed. 'What are you doing here?'

'Who is Clere?' Cindy muttered.

Zeta turned. 'It is my girlfriend. She has come to help us.'

They all jumped up. Cindy scowled.

'You never told me that you had a girlfriend,' she said.

They gathered around the door. The girl outside was shorter than Zeta by a head and had fine features and softly pointed ears. Incredibly, even by human standards, she was very pretty. Her hair was long and dark green. She did not seem surprised to see humans from Earth. She spoke mainly to her boyfriend.

'Zeta,' she said in a sad voice. 'I could not believe the news until now. Your uncle has put you in prison. Pray, what have you done wrong?'

'I have done nothing wrong,' Zeta said. 'Only I have discovered that Furma has struck an alliance with the Shadows in our fight with Gilbrare.'

Clere cringed. 'Can this be true? But they are monsters.'

Zeta nodded solemnly. 'It is unfortunate but true. And I suspect I am to be kept imprisoned until after the war is decided so that our people do not find out

108

the truth until too late. But I fear that by then the Shadows will have gained too much power. They could overrun our kingdom.'

'What can I do?' Clere asked.

'You have to get us out of here,' Zeta said. 'Speak to your father. He has known me a long time and trusts my judgement. Tell him the things I have seen in the Forbidden Territories. Duke Lester's people sharing wagons with Shadows. Tell him that my uncle has lost all sense of righteousness. This alliance will surely kill us all.'

Clere glanced at the humans. She frowned.

'Who are your friends?' she asked.

'It is a long story,' Zeta said. 'Just spread the word of what is happening and get us out of here. Once the truth reaches the people it will explode like fire blown by a strong wind. Then we will be safe from injustice.'

'The word will spread,' Watch warned. 'I just hope your King does not want to put out this particular fire with a hammer.'

Eleven

Watch's words proved prophetic. Two hours later they were out of the prison and fleeing the city of Centrae on horseback, in the direction of the mountain Zeta had spoken of. The peak that supposedly touched the sky. Fleeing was the correct word to describe their situation. The King had sent a small army after them. He even seemed to be leading it himself, if they could believe Zeta's superb vision. A gold and blue flag waved from the front of most horses. And Zeta thought he glimpsed Shadows riding alongside the King. Perhaps the rumours had already spread too far and the King had nothing left to hide.

Clere had done her job well. Her father must have been a powerful man in the kingdom. He had been able to send his own men past the King's guards. Yet his power must have had its limits. He had not been able to stop the King from going after them.

'I never thought I would see the day my uncle rode openly with the Shadows,' Zeta said as they paused at the crest of a tall hill. They were already halfway up the mountain, and if they could believe their own eyes, it looked as if they would touch the weird green sky soon. Clere sat on her horse beside Zeta.

'This is a sin,' Clere said. 'It must be stopped. No one hates us more than the Shadows.'

'If only we could be free of them,' Zeta said with a sigh.

'There could be a way,' Watch muttered.

'What are you thinking?' Cindy asked him.

'Many things,' Watch muttered. He gestured to the mountain top. But we'd better get up there before they reach us.'

The King and his army had superior horses, no

doubt the best in the land. They gained steadily on the gang as they strove to reach the sky. Yet it seemed that for once luck was finally on the gang's side. They rounded a sharp curve in the mountain path and suddenly ran into the sky.

It was like a huge dark sheet, hanging over their heads. Dismounting and climbing on to the top of the final slope, they poked at the sky. It was as hard as rock. Yet it felt more like plastic.

'This is a really weird place,' Sally muttered.

'How are we going to break through this?' Cindy asked Watch.

'And are we sure we won't find empty space on the other side?' Adam said. 'We might just find ourselves sucked out into a black vacuum.'

'I don't think we want to break through this sky,' Watch said. 'I think we want it to *open* for us. Specifically, open back in Spooksville.'

Sally stared up at the wide dark green canopy.

It seemed to stretch for ever, drooping low over the land.

'It doesn't look like we can just talk to it,' Sally said. 'How are we going to get it to open?'

'I have an idea,' Watch said with confidence.

Adam glanced back at the approaching army. King Furma definitely had plenty of Shadows with him. Maybe he intended to feed them to the beasts as punishment for upsetting his plans.

'Whatever you have planned, I think you had better do it now,' Adam told Watch.

Watch shrugged. 'I want to wait till the King gets here.'

'What?' the others cried in unison.

Watch held up his hand. 'I think I know how to solve the problem of the Shadows once and for all.'

'But it's not our problem,' Sally said. 'We are just kids, we should not get involved with their internal politics. We should get out of here while the going is good.'

'But if you could help us,' Clere said to Watch, and there was a note of pleading in her voice.

Zeta glanced at Cindy and his expression was worried.

'We need your help,' he said to her. 'But I don't know if we have the right to ask for it. I just know it would comfort me to know that you are safe.'

Cindy smiled. 'But I am not your concern.'

Zeta reached out his hand and squeezed her hand.

'You have become my concern,' he said sincerely.

Watch smiled at all the fuss, which he rarely did.

'There is no need to worry,' he said. 'We can defeat the Shadows and get home at the same time. In fact, the two things are related.'

'But how?' Adam asked.

'Think how we got here,' Watch said. 'We caused a rupture in the space-time continuum by concentrating fear on a particular place, which happened to be George's closet. In the same way it was only through another rupture – that was also made by fear – that the Shadow was able to enter Cindy's bedroom and steal her away. Fear is the key here. Fear keeps us trapped here in this realm. Fear makes this sky above us – this Curtain of Dreams – thick and impenetrable. But if we drop our fear I am sure we will be able to pass through it and back into our world as easily as we can swim through water.'

'Let's do it!' Sally exclaimed, as the army drew even closer. The King led the procession; he had already drawn his sword and there was no mis-taking the anger on his face. The Shadows at his back howled with glee, no doubt looking forward to plenty of human brains to eat.

'But how do we stop the Shadows?' Zeta asked Watch.

'The same way,' Watch said. 'Just don't be afraid of them. I believe, Zeta, Clere, that your people create these Shadows. That in this realm your fear has taken a physical body in the form of these monsters. Zeta, Cindy told me what you said about the Shadows. You said, "Some believe they come from the remains of our unconsumed fears." It was this clue that got me thinking along these lines.'

'But what exactly should we do about them now?' Zeta asked.

'Laugh at them, and I honestly believe they will vanish,' Watch said.

'This sounds like an extreme case of wishful thinking,' Sally muttered.

'What if they don't vanish?' Clere asked.

Watch shrugged. 'Then we are dead meat.'

Zeta considered and then spoke to the gang of humans.

'I think Watch might be right about how we can defeat the Shadows. But there is still a chance we might fail. For that reason I think you should leave this realm now, if you can.'

'A very logical and sound idea,' said Sally, climbing back up the slope.

'Wait,' Adam said to her. 'It is not like us to abandon friends.'

Cindy looked at Zeta and Clere. 'You risked your lives to save us,' she said. 'We are not leaving until we know you are safe.'

'You humans are more brave then I thought,' Zeta said with admiration.

'And more stupid,' Sally grumbled.

The army was on them in a minute. Flanked by Shadow guards, King Furma dismounted and strode up to Zeta. The young man stepped forward to meet him. Furma looked like a real King, even with his pointed ears and green skin. He was tall and powerfully built. On his head he wore a gold crown embedded with jewels.

But the King still held his sword and there was hatred in his eyes. Before saying a word he swept his blade to Zeta's throat, which made them all gasp. They had thought he was going to cut off Zeta's head. But Zeta himself did not flinch. He met his uncle's blazing stare and was not afraid. On both sides big ugly Shadows slobbered.

'Betrayed by my own blood!' the King cursed. 'I should take your life now and put an end to this rebellion. How could you do this to me?'

Zeta spoke calmly. 'How could you do this to your own people?'

'I made an alliance with the Shadows to save my people!'

Zeta still had the sword at his throat but that did not stop him from slowly shaking his head.

'You made this alliance to save yourself,' he said. 'Indeed, if you had not pushed Gilbrare so hard, demanded so many taxes and so much obedience, they would not have rebelled in the first place.'

'They are my subjects!' the King roared. 'They are to do as they are told! Like you were supposed to do what you were told!'

'It is true I am your subject,' Zeta said quietly. 'But I am also your nephew. And I do not believe you are so evil that you would just kill me. Even if I do intend to kill your evil plan.'

The King was haughty. 'You cannot stop my plan, Zeta.'

'But I can,' Zeta said.

Zeta turned to the nearby Shadows and laughed at them.

The Shadows froze as if stunned.

Sally was impressed. She pointed.

'Look at that,' she said. 'The laughter hurts them. Let's all laugh at them.'

The gang pointed at the Shadows and burst into hysterics, mocking the monsters at the same time.

'Ugly balls of green goo,' Sally said.

'Mindless beasts,' Watch said.

'Disgusting slobberers,' Adam said.

'Unpleasant companions,' Cindy said.

Sally turned to Cindy. 'That is not much of a criticism,' she said. 'Show a little fire.'

It did not matter. At their laughter, because of their absence of fear, the Shadows suddenly began to melt. To everyone's astonishment, once they started they couldn't stop. Soon, rather than having guards, the King had nothing but big pools of green goo. The King stared around in amazement, and in fear. He lowered his sword from Zeta's neck.

'You have destroyed my allies,' the King whispered.

'We have saved you from your real enemies,' Watch said. 'Your Highness, why don't you talk to the people of Gilbrare, reason with them? I am sure they don't want war any more than you do. It is way too much trouble, and people just end up getting hurt. I don't think you want that.'

The words had a strong effect on the King, or perhaps he was still recovering from the shock of seeing his guards melt. He stared at the humans as if seeing them for the first time, and the fear in his eyes was replaced by wonder. He turned back to his nephew.

'Forgive me for raising my sword to you, Zeta,' he said. 'That was unworthy. You are the only nephew I have.'

Zeta nodded. 'Forgive me for ever disobeying you.'

The King continued to study the humans. 'These are friends of yours, Zeta?' he asked.

Zeta nodded. 'I met them in the forbidden Territories. They are from Earth. They have come to our realm to help us.' He added, 'On earth they are considered great heroes.'

'That isn't exactly true but it sounds good,' Sally muttered.

King Furma nodded. 'I can see their greatness with my own eyes. They must be very powerful to defeat my army with their mere laughter. Their words are also wise. I will try to follow them, and make peace with Gilbrare. I am getting too old to fight anyway, and besides, I might not win without the Shadows at my back.' He paused. 'Would the humans like to remain in my kingdom, and be my personal guards?'

'We would enjoy that, King Furma,' Cindy spoke up. 'But it is Sunday back on Earth and we all have homework to do. But perhaps we can come back another time, when your problems with Gilbrare have been settled.'

'That is fine,' the King said. 'You have helped

open my eyes. I owe you a great debt. I grant you leave to be on your way.'

Watch and Adam turned their attention back to the sky.

It was only a few feet away but it looked as thick as ever.

'Now what do we do?' Adam muttered.

'Have faith and be fearless,' Watch said. Then he cupped his hands over his mouth and called out, 'Hey, Bryce? Tira? George? Are you guys there?'

Bryce answered from the other side of the sky.

'Yeah. We can hear you but we can't see you. Where are you?'

'Close,' Watch said. 'Are you still at George's?'

'Yeah. We're sitting in his closet. The rear of the closet began to glow with green light just before we heard you. Should we try to come through to where you are?'

'No,' Watch said. 'Just stick your arms through the light. You can help pull us through.'

'OK.'

A couple of human arms poked through the sky.

122

One looked like it belonged to Bryce, the other to Tira.

The gang was not surprised George had not stuck his arm through.

'This is a weird way to be saved,' Sally muttered. 'But as long as it works and we don't get stuck in the sky I don't care.'

'Don't even think about that,' Watch warned.

Cindy turned to Zeta and Clere and hugged them.

'This looks like goodbye,' she said. 'I am really happy I got to meet you both. Stay together always. You look like a cute couple.'

'Come back and see us soon,' Zeta said.

'We will miss you,' Clere said.

'I will return,' Cindy promised. Then she giggled. 'Some dark night when I am afraid to fall asleep!'

Exclusive watch for
Spooksville
fans!

Even Watch would be pleased to add this fantastic bubble watch to his collection! It's a digital time keeper with a difference! For one thing there's a special Spooksville bat floating around inside!

The watch is totally exclusive and can be yours for only £4.99 (incl. post and packing)

TAKE ADVANTAGE OF THIS SPECIAL OFFER. COLLECT SIX SPECIAL TOKENS AND CLAIM THE WATCH ABSOLUTELY FREE. COLLECT THREE TOKENS AND GET THE WATCH FOR ONLY £2.5

You'll find the tokens in special editions of Spooksville. Look for the flash on the cover